For our children Alexis and Jessica Kirschner and Travis and Rebecca Contreras.

May you always cherish the wonder of the written word.

The PAGEMASTER

David Kirschner & Ernie Contreras ~ Illustrations by Jerry Tiritilli

Kingfisher

Richard

ark, dangerous storm clouds filled the night sky. They shifted and twisted and swirled into terrible shapes—pirate ships, haunted houses, dragons. Lightning flashed! Thunder exploded! ❀ Ten-year-old Richard Tyler sprang up in his bed, gasping for breath. He could feel his heart pounding. It must be a dream, he told himself, just another bad dream. ❀ At this time of night, most ten-year-old boys were fast asleep, dreaming about things like playing baseball, riding bikes, and climbing trees. But Richard Tyler was not a typical ten-year-old. He dreamed about things like being struck by lightning, getting sucked into tornadoes, or falling into the Grand Canyon. ❀ To Richard the world was the scariest place imaginable. A dangerous place full of accidents waiting to happen. If a ten-year-old ever expected to make it to eleven, he'd better be prepared for these dangers. ❀ Richard fanned his emergency flashlight around his room, lighting up his fire extinguishers, his earthquake kits, and his crash helmets. The flashlight also lit up some of his favourite wall signs: NO SMOKING! . . . CAUTION! . . . BEWARE!

Looking out the window, he saw dark clouds near the horizon, somewhere beyond the town. Maybe he wasn't dreaming. Then suddenly, without any warning, lightning lit up the sky! Richard panicked. Grabbing one of his crash helmets, he ran out the door.

Hurrying down the hall, he headed for the safest place he knew—his parents' bedroom. As usual, the door was not quite shut. He was about to knock on it when he heard his parents talking.

"How can you say that?" his father was asking. "You know Richard is not a normal kid." Richard realised that they were talking about him. He took off his helmet and listened.

"Of course he's normal," his mother argued. "Every ten-year-old is afraid of something."

"Yeah, but every ten-year-old isn't afraid of everything," his father answered. "Claire, the boy is even afraid of tuna."

Wrong, Richard thought. He wasn't afraid of tuna. The high levels of mercury found in some tuna was what worried him. Richard peeked in through the crack in the doorway. His dad was looking out the window into the backyard, probably inspecting the tree house he was building. His dad was always trying to get Richard involved in high risk activities, like tree houses and Little League.

"Alan, the world is a frightening place for him right now," said his mother. "I think that last earthquake was just too much for him. Right now we need to be as supportive as possible."

"Supportive? I'm running out of supportive things to do. I signed him up for Little League and he drove the team crazy with statistics about shin splints leading to blood clots in the legs. He even brought in medical evidence. No one wanted to play after that."

Richard watched his father walk away from the window and plop down on the big bed. He had a hopeless look on his face. "I just want to be a good father, Claire. That's all."

Suddenly Richard saw his problems from his parents' point of view. He no longer felt like going into their room.

Back in his own room, Richard sank down on his bed. The beam from his flashlight created a circle of light on the ceiling. It reminded him of a full moon. Then he remembered that statistics showed that violent crimes increase during full moons. Probably werewolves did, too. As far as Richard was concerned, no one had ever disproved the existence of werewolves. His heart beat faster at the thought, and he fanned the flashlight under his bed just in case. . . . No werewolves there—just a life preserver and two more earthquake kits.

As he crawled under the covers, he began to think about his dad again. Richard really didn't want to be a disappointment to him. Starting tomorrow he'd try to act more like a normal kid. But that wasn't going to be easy!

The next morning Richard hurried over to the window to see how much destruction the storm had caused. He didn't expect to see many houses still standing. To his amazement the whole neighbourhood had been spared. The lightning hadn't destroyed a single house.

Richard stared out the window at the green lawns, the colourful gardens, and the pretty houses. It was a nice neighbourhood, he thought. But what did that prove? Even in the nicest neighbourhoods, danger could lurk around every corner.

He watched a cluster of bike-riding kids race around the corner onto his street. They were pedalling at full speed into driveways and jumping their bikes off the curb. They called it "catching air" when both wheels left the ground. The way they all wooed and yahooed and slapped high fives, you would think they had just found a cure for the common cold.

Watching from the safety of his room,

Richard figured there would be no less than three broken legs, two cracked heads, and one ruptured spleen. He was all ready to call 999. If the emergency line was busy, he could help out himself. After all, he was certified in first aid, CPR, and the Heimlich manoeuvre.

But no one fell. He guessed that some kids were just lucky that way.

To please his father, Richard decided to take an interest in the tree house he was building. Not that he really had any interest in it, but he would try to act as if he did if it would make his dad happy. He pushed open the screen door and walked out into the messy backyard. Pieces of wood and tools were scattered around the tree house construction area. Plenty of safety violations there, Richard noticed.

"How's it goin', Dad?" Richard looked up into the tree house where his dad was hammering away.

His father was surprised to hear the boy's voice. "Richard!" he shouted. "How do you like it?" His dad gestured around the tree house like a tour guide.

"Uh, it looks great." Actually, to Richard it looked like a bunch of boards that the wind might have blown into the tree branches. But his dad seemed pleased by the compliment.

"Hey, Rich. How about bringing up that bag of nails?" His dad pointed down to a paper bag next to Richard's feet.

"Uh, sure." Richard lifted the bag and held it up over his head.

"Nah, c'mon up. The view is terrific," his dad said.

Though Richard wanted to please his father, he couldn't ignore the obvious. He pointed at the ladder. "Dad, eight percent of all household accidents involve ladders. And another three percent involve trees. You're dealin' with an eleven percent probability. I'll just stay on the ground if you don't mind."

"I give up," he heard his dad mumble. "Just hand me the nails."

Richard held the bag as high as he could, and his dad reached down as far as he could. Unfortunately his dad reached a little too far. His feet slid down the ladder and he crashed face first into the grass.

Richard's mum ran out of the house and hurried over to her husband. "Honey, are you all right?" Richard's father couldn't answer immediately. He was too busy spitting large clumps of grass and dirt out of his mouth.

"I tried to warn him about the ladder." Richard shook his head.

His dad picked up the bag of nails and reached inside. There were only a few left. He turned toward his son. "Rich, here's something you can do." He placed a nail in Richard's hand. "Go down to Guttman's Hardware and pick up a pound of these nails."

Richard turned to his mother. "Mum? Do I have to?"

His mother knelt down beside him. "Richie, Guttman's is just a short bike ride into town."

"B-but most traffic accidents happen within three blocks of the home."

"Rich, you can't base your whole life on statistics. You've got to take some chances once in a while," his father said. He stuffed a five dollar bill into the boy's clenched fist.

"This is not good. Not good at all," Richard muttered as he headed for the garage.

A few minutes later, the automatic garage door jerked open with a loud bang. There sat Richard balancing on his bike. He looked like some creature from outer space. On his head he wore a hockey helmet equipped with multiple reflectors and rear-view mirrors. A yellow jacket streaked with green fluorescent tape covered the upper part of his body.

His bike was outfitted with every accessory ever designed for biking safety: lights, reflectors, mirrors, fenders, horns, bells, basket, fire extinguisher, and earthquake and first aid kits.

So far Richard hadn't figured out how to install an air bag, but he was working on it.

He grunted as he pushed off down the driveway. With all its safety devices, the bike was heavier than a Volvo. It wobbled slowly across the sidewalk and off into the road—and the dangerous unknown.

As the bike bounced and wobbled up the quiet street, Richard kept his eyes wide open for any possible danger. At every intersection he stopped and looked carefully in all four directions. He was so busy looking for any sign of dangerous traffic that he failed to see the dark storm clouds gathering behind him.

Turning a corner, he met up with the same kids he'd seen earlier riding their bikes. They had constructed a ramp—a wooden plank propped up on a stack of cinder blocks. The kids were catching "major air" off the ramp.

Richard thought of turning back before he was noticed.

"Hey, check it out!" One of the kids shouted at the top of his lungs. "It's Richie Tyler!"

"Look what he's wearin'!"

"Yeah, where ya goin', Tyler, the moon?" The kids skidded one-eighties on both sides

of the ramp, forming a bike blockade across the street. The only way for Richard to get through was over the ramp.

"C'mon, Tyler, catch some air!"

"Go for it!"

But Richard wasn't about to try anything as dangerous as that. He turned his bike around and pedalled off in the opposite direction. He heard the kids laughing behind him. At this point Richard really wanted to go home, but he couldn't disappoint his dad by returning home empty-handed. He decided to turn down a side street even if it meant taking a longer, scarier way into town.

A strong wind began to blow, and the lonely street got darker. Glancing up at the sky, Richard spotted the threatening black storm clouds. There was a bright flash of lightning followed by a loud crack of thunder. Then came the rain, pouring down in thick, driving sheets. Richard had to find shelter—fast!

He pedalled frantically into the park, steering his bike down a wet, tree-lined path. A violent blast of wind snapped a thick branch from a tree. It fell across his path. Richard swerved to avoid the branch and crashed, helmet-first, into the concrete base of a statue. Flying off the bike, he hit the ground with a

thud. He took off his helmet and felt his head for injuries.

There was another brilliant flash of lightning. Richard looked up at the big bronze statue of the town's founding father. The huge metal figure was pointing off toward a big stone building at the end of the park. Richard decided to go where the statue was pointing. Leaving his bike and his helmet behind, he scrambled to his feet and ran for the building as fast as his legs could carry him.

The building was huge. Across the front there were marble columns the size of giant redwoods. Marble steps led up to a tall oak door, and a pair of ferocious-looking lion statues guarded both sides of the entrance.

Richard ran up the steps, trying not to look at the fierce lions. He pulled the tall oak door toward him and stepped inside. The door swung closed, pushing Richard forward. Though he was surrounded by darkness, Richard sensed that he was standing in a huge, cavernous room. He couldn't imagine what dangers might be hidden there. Blood-sucking bats? Man-eating monsters? Poisonous snakes? Or perhaps there was a crypt, where mummies were buried.

Suddenly he panicked. He wanted to get out. But as he turned to exit, he noticed a long rectangle of light reflected on the dark floor. It was coming from an open door where a strange and hideous black creature was standing. All at once the creature lunged for-

ward toward Richard. It was grunting and breathing heavily.

Richard tried to run but his wet sneakers slipped on the smooth floor. He stumbled backwards into a wall. Escape was impossible. Richard shut his eyes tightly and waited for the end.

Then he heard a man's voice echoing in the darkness. "That's some storm out there." Richard opened one eye, then the other. Standing in the rectangle of light, the creature turned out to be just an old man carrying a stack of books. He placed the books on a nearby desk, then reached for a light panel on the wall. As he clicked the switches one by one, long rows of sparkling chandeliers lighted up, revealing a vast space filled with rows upon rows of books, whole walls of books stretching as far as the eye could see.

"Welcome to the library, my young friend." The old man took out a handkerchief and wiped his brow. "I'm the librarian, Mr. Dewey." Mr. Dewey offered his handkerchief to Richard, whose face was wet from the rain. In fact, there were pools of water where he stood.

"No, no thanks," Richard said, fearing that the old man's handkerchief might be filled with germs. He was careful not to take his eyes off the strange old librarian.

Mr. Dewey's hair grew straight up out of his head like white grass. And his face had more wrinkles than his dirty old white handkerchief. But his eyes were sharp and clear. They spark-

lod as if they knew things that no one else knew. Mr. Dewey leaned in close to Richard.

"I expect you're here for a special book."

Book? "M-mister, I just need a . . . "

"Wait!" Mr. Dewey gestured for Richard to be quiet. "Allow me to guess. I have a talent for guessing what people need."

Richard was afraid that the old man might become violent, so he let him have his way.

"I know you're in need of a . . . fantasy! Brave knights, mythical fairies, ferocious drag-ons, damsels in distress." Mr. Dewey raised his bushy eyebrows.

Richard shook his head. "No. . . . Look, all I want is . . . "

"Adventure! Of course! You're a boy who loves adventure. You must be to have braved a horrible storm like this." Mr. Dewey glanced up toward the rain-soaked windows. "Adven-ture! Brimming with wicked villains, buried treasure, and dirty cutthroat pirates." He drew his finger across his neck to illustrate his words.

Richard massaged his throat. "N-no, that's not it."

Lightning flooded the high windows. Mr. Dewey poked his face up to Richard's. "Horror! Evil demons, wretched monsters, haunted houses, graveyards." He wrung his hands and licked his lips like Quasimodo, the famous hunchback of Notre Dame.

Richard gulped, too terrified to speak.

"Yes, it's horror for you, boy. I'm sure of it." Mr. Dewey held out his hand. "Your library card, please."

"Uh, I don't have one."

"Don't have a library card?" The old man looked amazed. "Well, now you do."

Mr. Dewey suddenly produced a library card from between his fingers and placed it on the desk next to Richard. "Sign there. Last name first." Richard did as he was told.

Mr. Dewey picked up the card and held it close to his eyes. "Richard Tyler." He proudly handed the card to Richard. "Mr. Tyler, consider this your passport through the wonderful —and quite unpredictable—world of books."

"But I'm not here for any books." Richard felt relieved that he had finally got the words out. "That's what I've been trying to tell you. I just came in because of the storm."

"You mean you don't need? . . . " Mr. Dewey was disappointed. "Oh, I see."

"Is there a phone I can use to call my parents?" Richard looked around.

Mr. Dewey shook his head and sighed as if he had lost something of great value. Then he pointed off into the library, saying, "Through there." Richard looked in the direction Mr. Dewey's finger was pointing, but he saw nothing except endless rows of book stacks.

"Proceed in a northeasterly direction and continue on to the rotunda," the old man explained. "From the rotunda head west through the fiction section. There you will find the public telephone. You can't miss it."

Richard walked up toward the book stacks. The aisles seemed to go on forever. He might never find his way out of here. His knees began to shake.

"Don't be afraid, boy." Mr. Dewey's voice echoed in the huge room. "If you lose your way, merely direct yourself back to the EXIT sign."

Richard looked back. Mr. Dewey was pointing toward the glowing green exit sign high over the big oak doors. This was hopeful, Richard thought. An exit sign meant there was a possibility of escape.

Just as another clap of thunder rumbled overhead, Richard cautiously took his first step into the unknown.

Back home, Richard's mum stared out the window at the pouring rain. She would have given anything to see her son ride his crazy-looking bike up the driveway.

Richard's dad was on the phone. "C'mon . . ." he was muttering to himself. This was not the time to be on hold. "H-hello? Mr. Guttman? . . .

This is Alan Tyler. My son, Richard, is he there? . . . Yeah, that's him, the kid with the earthquake kits. . . . You haven't seen him?" The disappointment was evident in his voice. "Please call if he comes in. Thank you." He turned to his wife. "He never got there."

Hanging up the phone, he grabbed his keys from the coffee table. "I'm going out to find him," he said, and bolted out the front door into the pouring rain.

"I'm coming with you!" Richard's mum grabbed two coats from the rack beside the door and ran out after her husband.

Book stacks shot up on each side of Richard like skyscrapers. Every once in a while he glanced back to check on the exit sign. It was still there. Finally he stepped out from an aisle into a wide-open circular space. He must have reached the rotunda—the centre of the library. There all the sections came together.

A cut-marble image of a compass was inlaid into the floor. Now which way did Mr. Dewey say the phone was: north, south, east, or west? Richard looked in every direction, searching for a clue. Finally he looked up.

"Geeeezzz!" He was standing directly under the big dome of the huge library building. Spanning the curved surface of the dome was an amazing mural. It included, in brilliant colours, some of the greatest heroes and villains of classic fiction. Richard recognised the pirate Long John Silver, the two-faced Dr. Jekyll and Mr. Hyde, and the Frankenstein monster.

In the centre of the mural the artist had painted the image of a wizened old man. He wore a long white beard and clutched a book edged in shimmering gold. His sharp eyes stared down at Richard like an eagle eyeing its prey.

B-A-N-G! A clap of thunder rattled the book stacks. Richard jumped back in surprise. Once again his wet sneakers slipped out from underneath him. As he fell backwards, his head hit the hard and unforgiving marble floor. Then . . . Everything went black.

When Richard came to, he was lying flat on his back in the centre of the rotunda floor. Everything was pitch black. He expected Mr. Dewey to snap the switches again and bring back the light. But the darkness remained.

"H-hello?" he said, hoping that someone would answer. But his voice came back with a hollow echo, "Lo?-lo?-lo?-lo? . . . " A cold icicle of fear shot up his spine, and he looked for the exit sign. It was nowhere in sight. Not good, he thought. Not good at all.

Lightning flashed through the high windows again, lighting up the rotunda dome. Instinctively, Richard looked up and gasped in terror. Was he really seeing what he thought he saw—shadows climbing out of the mural? A second flash of lightning confirmed his fears. The painted images had come to life and were climbing down the rotunda columns!

Then Richard heard footsteps coming from the shadows around him. Terrified, he scrunched

down, with his head between his legs.

In the darkness he sensed that something was hovering over him. He could hear it breathing. He looked up. A tall, shadowy figure stood before him. "M-Mr. Dewey?"

A sudden flash of lightning spotlighted an old man with a long white beard. He was wearing an amazing cloak made out of book pages. In one hand he held a beautifully carved staff; in the other a large book edged in gold.

"W-who're you?" Richard asked. The figure took a step backward and Richard gasped. "You're that guy from up there!" he said, pointing up toward the mural, which now had no figures in it.

"I am the Pagemaster." The voice was deep and smooth. "Keeper of the books and guardian of the written word." The Pagemaster bowed low before Richard. As he bent over the pages on his cloak rustled like dried leaves.

"Where're the other guys?" Richard hoped that Frankenstein wasn't lurking in the shadows.

"Why, they're here of course—all around us." The Pagemaster gestured with his staff. A magical swirl of light seemed to flow out of the end of his staff, illuminating the space.

"L-listen, Mr. Pagemaster. I really gotta go now." Richard looked around in confusion. All the aisles looked exactly alike. "Maybe you could show me the way out?"

"If that is what you truly want."

"Yes, it is." Richard said as he vigorously

shook his head up and down in agreement.

"Splendid!" The Pagemaster spun around and walked across the rotunda. "Follow me."

"This is the way out?" Richard asked nervously.

The Pagemaster stopped, turning back toward Richard. "It is the only way," he answered very seriously. Then, with his staff he pointed up to a sign, FICTION A-Z, which hung over a section of the book stacks.

"Fiction A to Z! Where all is possible!" The Pagemaster lifted his arms, and the gold-edged pages of his cloak shimmered like a moonlit waterfall. "The place where a child's imagination can take root and grow to incredible heights!" He plucked a book page off his cloak and flung it high into the air. The page fluttered up and magically transformed itself into a giant! Richard hid behind the Pagemaster's cloak as the giant turned and stomped off, shaking the ground with his heavy steps.

The Pagemaster turned to Richard. "Fiction A to Z, where a child's courage is the wind that moves him to discovery!" The Pagemaster flicked another page up over the book stacks. From out of an aisle, a Viking ship sailed forth, gliding through the air, its oars sweeping it forward through the rotunda. Richard ducked for his life as the ship passed overhead.

The Pagemaster knelt before Richard, pointing into the fiction section. "This is where your journey begins!" he said. And with a sudden swirl of his staff, the Pagemaster started a

book cart moving toward Richard from behind.

"Can we go now?" Richard asked. But the words were barely out of his mouth when the cart hit him from behind. It knocked him backward into the cart, which then circled around the rotunda picking up speed. Suddenly it whipped off into the aisle under the fiction sign.

"Godspeed to you, boy!" The Pagemaster called. "And remember—when in doubt look to the boooooooks!" The Pagemaster's voice echoed across the library.

Richard held on tight as the book cart raced through the fiction aisles—faster and faster and faster! The endless rows of books passed by in a blur. Then he heard a loud, strange noise—a weird mixture of wind, fluttering pages, and voices. The voices were quoting phrases from books: "Once upon a time . . ." "Long ago and far away . . ." "All for one and one for all . . ." "Call me Ishmael . . ." "Please, sir, may I have some more . . ." "All my pirates share the grave . . ."

Then Richard caught sight of a telephone booth at the end of the aisle. His cart was rushing directly toward it. He tried to stop, but the cart had no brakes. It crashed smack into the telephone booth, sending Richard head over heels onto a pile of books.

As the boy began to regain his senses, his eyes focused on the telephone receiver, which was swinging back and forth just above his nose. He grabbed the receiver. A prerecorded voice fil-

tered through the line: "Due to the storm all lines have been temporarily disconnected."

"Oh, great!" he said. "That's just great."

Suddenly the books under him rumbled and shook. An earthquake? Richard screamed as a fifteen-centimetre sword slashed up from under the books, just missing his right leg.

He watched in terror as a scrappy old book scrambled up from under the pile, grumbling and cursing. It had all the trimmings of a pirate: eyepatch, bandanna, peg leg, and a hook for a hand. On its cover, large, ornate tattoo-like letters indicated that its name was ADVENTURE.

"Where's the son of a rum puncheon who knocked the wind from me sails? Where's 'e be? Where's 'e be?" The adventure book ruffled its pages like a dog shaking its wet fur.

Richard was too shocked to speak.

Suddenly the adventure book spotted him. "Ya ha!" the book shouted, leaping onto the telephone receiver and swinging there like a pirate in the rigging of a ship. "So here be the lubber 'at scuffed me covers and with no apologies, too. I've got half a notion to cut out yer tongue and use it fer a bookmark."

Richard shut his eyes tight. "I'm dreaming. I'm dreaming," he kept chanting.

"I ain't no dream, boy." Adventure jabbed his sword at Richard's nose. "You fiction er non-fiction?"

"I'm Ri-Ri-Richard. Ri-Richard T-Tyler."

Adventure squinted his good eye. "Ri-

22

Richard T-Tyler. What kind o' book would that be?"

"I'm n-not a book." Richard's voice cracked with fear.

"Got any proof?"

Richard frantically searched his pockets for identification. He found the library card. "See? Here's my name." Richard held up the card.

Adventure lifted his eyepatch to study the card with both eyes. "Don't really need this eyepatch," he grumbled, "but no self-respecting pirate would be caught dead without one."

"It is a library card!" Adventure shouted in surprise. He lowered his sword and respectfully removed the bandanna from his head. "Beggin' yer pardon, lad. Didn't know ye was a customer." Smiling widely, he exposed a mouthful of broken teeth.

Richard didn't want anything to do with this grungy pirate adventure book. "L-look," he protested: "I just wanna get outta here."

"Of carse ya do, matey! We all do!" Adventure gestured around with his sword at the endless rows of books.

Richard scrambled to his feet and tried to escape down the aisle. "J-just stay away from me," he cried.

Adventure lodged his sword between his teeth and leapt onto a nearby ladder, the kind that rolls. He gave a shove with his peg leg, and the ladder took off down the aisle.

Richard looked nervously for the exit sign. "What happened to it?" he asked himself.

"That's what I was meanin' to talk to ye about, mate!" Adventure, still on the rolling ladder, pulled up next to Richard. "I know these here waters like the back of me hand," Adventure said. He demonstrated by holding his hook in the air.

Richard didn't trust Adventure. "Uh . . . thanks, but I think I can find my own way out," he said, continuing down the aisle. He wanted to get rid of the pushy book.

Adventure called out. "This is a library, mate. Lots o' surprises!"

Richard glanced back to make sure Adventure wasn't following. This proved to be a bad idea, for he fell right through a hole in the library floor.

"Eeeeeooooooww!" Richard screamed as he tumbled down into a deep, dark pit with a pool of black water at the bottom. Just as he was expecting to hit the water with a big splash, a huge anchor swung down and caught him between the legs. The anchor began to swing back and forth across the pit.

Suddenly Richard heard a strange noise. It sounded like a clock ticking. But what would a clock be doing down here? He soon found out. A giant alligator shot up out of the water and opened its powerful jaws, ready to snap at him. Looking down, Richard saw that an old alarm clock was wedged inside its throat. Could this be the alligator from *Peter Pan*?

Just in time, the anchor began to pull him up, away from the water—and the alligator.

Richard breathed a sigh of relief. Help had finally arrived. He jumped off and collapsed on the library floor. Standing over him was his smiling rescuer, Adventure.

"W-what happened?" Richard asked.

"As ye can see, mate, not everything's as it seems." Adventure glanced around suspiciously.

"This place is dangerous," Richard whispered. In desperation, he turned to Adventure. "You know the way out?"

Adventure grinned. "Why, sure I do, matey. I'd be happy t'navigate ye outta here. But there's one small favour I might be askin' in return."

"Favour? What kind of favour?"

"Well, I'm afeard I've been dry-docked in this library far longer than I'd like t'remember. I need t'breathe the open air again and feel a fair wind against me pages. As I sees it, you are me ticket outta here. Is it a deal, mate?"

"You want me to check you out?"

"That's right! Yer a bright lad, ye are."

"O-okay. Can we go now?"

"Aye-aye!" Adventure saluted with his hook. "Let's scale this mast and get our bearings."

"That's not a mast," Richard protested. "That's a ladder. I don't like ladders. I kinda have this thing about heights." Richard produced a very weak smile.

"Ye do, do ye?" Adventure smoothed his moustache with his hook. This seemed to show he was thinking. He reached into a book stack and pulled out a book called *20,000 Leagues Under the Sea*. When he opened it, the book started to rumble and shake. Adventure flung it on the floor just as a raging funnel of sea water blasted out from its pages.

Richard backed into the ladder. As he watched in horror, a slimy, giant squid tentacle squirmed from between the pages of the book. Richard scrambled up the ladder faster than a fireman. Adventure climbed up beside him.

"What'd you do that for?" Richard turned to Adventure angrily. "You're supposed to be helping me!"

"I am helpin' ya. I'm helpin' ya find the exit." Adventure removed his peg leg. With three clicks he gradually stretched it out into a telescope. "We'll just have a look-see," he explained. Placing the telescope over his eye, he scanned the territory.

Still clinging tightly to the top of the ladder, Richard slowly raised up to look over the top of the book stacks. Nothing had prepared him for the amazing sight he saw there.

Laid out before him, like an incredible tapestry, the greatest stories of all time had come to life. Amazing sights and sounds were coming from every direction. "Thar she blows!" a lookout shouted from the crow's-nest of a clipper ship, as it glided between the stacks.

Nearby a magnificent white whale jumped upward, then crashed back down, sending an explosion of water up into the air. Suddenly the boiling white water transformed itself into a cloudy mist, which moved across a full yellow moon, then dipped down to surround

a scary old house. A bolt of lightning high-lighted a tall tower that rose high above the house. A shadowy swarm of bats came flying out of it.

Richard ducked as the bats flew over his head in a blind flurry. When he turned to watch them fly off, they turned into huge pterodactyls! The giant, leather-winged pre-historic creatures circled slowly above a volcano that erupted in explo-sions of hot, orange-coloured lava and black smoke.

Looking in another dir-ection, Richard spied a boy in a white turban, perched aboard a flying carpet. He was swooping and gliding around the tall minarets of ancient Baghdad. Then, above the distant horizon, an odd green-ish light appeared. Richard pushed up his glasses and strained for a better look. Abruptly, he snatched the telescope away from Adventure and slowly brought the green glow into focus. "I see it! I see it!" the boy shouted. Through the lens of the telescope, Richard had spotted the precious exit sign.

Just then the ladder started to shake. Richard gave Adventure an angry look. "Hey! Stop messing with the ladder!"

"Don't tell me." Adventure pointed down. "Tell him!" Not far from the end of Adven-ture's finger, a giant squid tentacle was begin-ning to slowly weave its way up the ladder.

"Ahhhhhhh!" Richard screamed.

Adventure snatched back his peg and leapt across the aisle to the opposite stack. Catch-ing a shelf with his hook, he swung himself up. "Jump, boy!" he shouted back at Richard.

But Richard was too frightened to move. He had climbed the ladder as far as he could. If he tried to go back down, the giant squid would get him.

"Jump!" Adventure barked out from across the aisle.

"I can't," Richard screamed. "It's too dangerous."

"It's either jump or your life," Adventure replied.

Richard felt a slimy squid tentacle wrap itself around his foot. Desper-ately he tried to kick it off. But the tentacle was pulling him down! In his panic he kicked the shelf, and the ladder began to roll away from the book stack and fall toward the other side of the aisle.

"Whoooooaaa!" Richard smashed into the opposite stack. Though he scrambled to stay on the ladder, he only managed to grab a book, which slid right off the shelf. Both Richard and the book started to fall. But instead of crashing to the ground, Richard suddenly seemed to be floating through the air. The book he was holding had sprouted wings and was gently lowering him to the floor.

The book did not look happy. Richard's

hand was planted firmly over its mouth, muffling a barrage of strangled threats. The book shook its small fists and kicked its little glass-slippered feet in protest.

Richard let go. The book gasped a few times, trying to catch its breath. Then it began to scold. "What do you think you're doing grabbing me like that!"

Richard looked up. Hovering just above him was an angry fairy book, complete with

wand, crown, and pixie dust. Scripted in glitter on the side of her satin cover was the title, FANTASY. "W-well, I was just . . ." Richard stammered.

"A likely story." Fantasy fluttered down to the ground. Yanking up her drooping bloomers, she smoothed out her clothes.

Richard watched in astonishment. "Who're you?"

"Who do I look like—the tooth fairy?"

"Well . . ."

"Don't answer that," she ordered. Using her wand as a pencil, she spelled out her name in the air with pixie dust.

Richard read aloud. "Fan-ta-sy."

"Oh, you can read. How refreshing." The pixie dust spilled onto the floor. Now Fantasy used her wand as a vacuum to suck back the shimmering dust. "You wouldn't believe how expensive this stuff is," she explained.

She looked down and noticed Richard's card on the ground. "What have we here?" She picked up the card and examined it. "A library card! Why, I haven't seen one of these in . . . well . . . a long time." She glanced up at Richard.

"Look, I gotta go." Richard started to move down the aisle. "Somebody was showing me the way out and I think I kinda lost him."

Fantasy fluttered in front of Richard. "Not so fast. Tell me. What's the one thing that you wish for more than anything in the world?"

That was easy. Richard wished he could make his father proud of him. But he figured the fairy probably wasn't offering miracles, so he decided to ask for something more practical. "Right now I'd settle for getting out of here."

"Honey, I'll grant your wish. But you've got to do me one small kindness in return."

"What is it?"

Fantasy grabbed Richard's collar in desperation. "You gotta check me outta here! I've been on that shelf so long my wings are wilting!"

"That's easy," Richard thought. "Okay," he said. "What are we waitin' for!" He stood up straight, pressed his hands to his side, and shut his eyes tight. But nothing happened. He squinted one eye open and looked at Fantasy. "Do I have to click my heels or something?"

Fantasy shook her head. "Honey, you're in the wrong story. Did you think you were in Oz?"

High above them, Adventure was climbing over the top of a book stack. He spied Richard talking to Fantasy. "Hold on there, sister!" Adventure shouted. "The lad's with me!"

"Do you know that short story?" Fantasy asked Richard.

"Yeah, he's Adventure."

"Honey, that's what they all say."

"I heard that!" Adventure was furious. "I'll have ye' know I'm a classic!"

"A classic misprint!" Fantasy shouted back.

"Why you old sea hag! I'll rip out yer pages and use them fer . . ." Adventure slipped off the book stack, screaming, "Maaaateeeeeeey!"

Richard turned to Fantasy. "Do something!"

"Oh, all right." Fantasy whirled her wand like a major league pitcher getting ready to throw a ball. Then she flicked it right at the falling Adventure. But the wand had no effect at all. Adventure splattered down onto the floor.

"Oops. I forgot. My wand doesn't work outside the Fantasy section," Fantasy said with a mischievous grin.

"You mean you can't wish me to the exit?" Richard's tone of voice showed his disappointment at this news.

Adventure picked himself up and ruffled his pages. "I'll bet she's never even seen the exit. Not once since she's been here!"

Fantasy fluttered up nose to nose with Adventure. "I've seen it more than you have, shorty. The exit's just beyond my fantasy section. I can see it from the very top of Rapunzel's tower."

"Then what're ye doin' in these parts?" Adventure was still annoyed at her.

"I've been misshelved. But that's all over now that this young Prince Charming has come to check me out." Fantasy grabbed Richard's arm and pulled him away.

"My good eye he is! The lad's checkin' me out!" Adventure grabbed Richard's other arm. "C'mon, boy." Adventure started to pull Richard off in the opposite direction.

Fantasy took a deep breath, swelling up her pages. Then she clapped them shut! A blast of pixie dust sprayed into Adventure's face.

"Ah . . . ahh . . . ahhh . . . choooo!" A man-sized sneeze shot him backwards into a book stack. "Oooomph!"

Adventure was sprawled upside down against a book stack. Glaring at the fairy book, he grumbled away to himself. "Fantasy. Ha! She's a nightmare."

Fantasy nudged Richard down the aisle. "C'mon, honey. That old adventure book's no help. He doesn't even know where we are now."

Adventure hopped up. "Bilge water! O' course I know where we are. We're . . ."

Adventure had to think fast because actually he didn't have the slightest idea where they were. Turning to the bookshelf, he pulled out a book entitled, *The Hound of the Baskervilles.*

"We're in Baskervilles," he shouted. "Have a look-see." He handed the book to Richard. Without thinking, Richard opened it. A huge, snarling dog's head thrust out from inside the pages. Richard screamed and tossed the book to Fantasy, who tossed it to Adventure. Not having anyone else to toss it to, Adventure dropped it on the floor. The mad dog was

beginning to pull itself from out of the book.

"Run!" Richard shouted.

Together they took off down the aisle in a screaming panic. Richard stumbled over a book cart, sending a batch of books flying into the air. One of the books flipped open as it hit the floor. Gunshots rang out. A posse of cowboys galloped up out of the pages and took over the chase from the hound.

Richard ducked as bullets whizzed overhead. One bullet hit a book and knocked it off the shelf. It fell open. There was a loud blast from a steam whistle. Then a full-size train suddenly charged up out of the book, filling the aisle with steam and sparks. ORIENT EXPRESS was printed on the side of the engine.

Richard and his friends ducked around a corner—right into a dead end. The train was headed straight for them! Terrified, Richard leaned back against the stack. There seemed to be no escape. Accidentally, his hand pushed in a book. This caused the bookcase to swing around. In a flash they escaped from one aisle into another, even stranger world.

Horror

full moon cast a grey light over an eerie graveyard. Chills ran up Richard's spine. He'd never been in a graveyard at night. He'd never been in a graveyard, period. "A-are we still in the library?" Richard stammered. "Aye, the horror section." Adventure drew his sword. "It looks pretty scary." Richard's knees were shaking. "That it does. Jest stick close to me an' ye got nothin' to worry 'bout." Adventure stepped forward. "Boy, do I feel safe now," Fantasy said sarcastically. Adventure's sword led the way through the graveyard. A blast of wind scattered a pile of dried leaves across their path, startling Richard. He jumped back into a pile of books—which weren't books at all, but bats! The swarm ignited into a frenzy, flapping and squeaking as they flew up into the air. "Get away from me, you flying rats!" Fantasy beat the bats back with her wand. As she turned around, Fantasy chuckled to herself when she spied Adventure cradled in Richard's arms. He looked exactly like a frightened baby.

Adventure scrambled down. "I was merely leapin' to the boy's protection," he explained.

"Uh-huh." Fantasy replied. "And Sleeping Beauty was an insomniac."

They continued on past a fog-layered gully and up a hill covered with old gravestones.

"There it is!" Richard shouted. He was pointing toward the exit sign hovering in the distant sky. Unfortunately, the sign was directly above a very scary-looking house. Probably haunted, Richard thought.

"Looks like the only way to reach the exit is through that thar house." Adventure didn't look too happy either.

"No way I'm going in there." Richard sounded as if he meant it.

Fantasy looked around at the tall, smooth cliffs that surrounded them. "I'm afraid there's no other way out," she said.

"It's yer only chance, boy." Adventure tried to persuade Richard. "C'mon. It's jest a house."

Just a house, Richard thought. Doesn't he know that seventeen percent of all accidents happen in the house?

Cautiously they approached the old iron gate that fronted the property. The house was much bigger and scarier than Richard had thought. Tall, windows stared out onto the porch, and a high tower rose from the centre of the house. While Richard was staring at the spooky old mansion, Adventure pushed the gate open with his sword. It fell off its hinges and crashed to the ground. They kept on going,

climbing the creaking stairs up to the porch.

"What's that?" Richard pointed to an iron chain hanging from the upper part of the house.

"The bell would be my guess," said Fantasy.

"Go on, lad. Ring it." Adventure was too short to reach the chain. Richard grabbed hold of it and gave a yank. CLANG! CLANG!

From out of the upper shadows of the house something fell down, splattering onto the porch. It was a hideous book creature. Richard and Adventure had the same reaction. "Aaa-aahh!" they shrieked.

The creature was as terrified as they were. It let out a bloodcurdling scream, too. Although it wasn't a monster, it certainly wasn't pleasant to look at. Like Adventure and Fantasy, it was a living book. But this book was in pitiful shape. Its spine was twisted and its face was hideous. The name HORROR was scratched in red on its shredded cover.

Adventure bravely stepped in front of Richard and drew his sword. "Stand back, boy. I'll give this hunchbook a taste of adventure!"

"Sanctuary! Sanctuary!" The horror book

cried. He scrambled up the bell chain and hid behind the moulding over the doorway.

"Come on down, ya dog-eared scallywag!" Adventure jabbed his sword up toward the hidden book.

"Oh, put that thing away. You're frightening him," Fantasy said as she fluttered up to the top of the door. "Come out, come out wherever you are!" Fantasy sang in her most motherly voice.

A sad, childlike voice cut through the darkness. "No! I know why you screamed. It's because I'm . . . I'm . . . h-horrible. I scared you."

"Hey, do I look scared?" Fantasy was buffing her fingernails.

"You're not scared?" Horror's crooked head rose above the opening.

"Course not." She offered her hand. "Come on down."

"Na-uh. No." Horror pointed down at Adventure. "He wants to hurt me."

"Him?" Fantasy dismissed Adventure with a gesture. "That little guy can't hurt anybody but himself. C'mon down."

Horror studied Fantasy. He decided that she looked very friendly. "Okay," he said, stepping out onto the moulding. He reached out . . . and lost his balance. Down he went, screaming again.

This time Horror landed in Richard's arms. "Here, take him!" Richard held the book out to Fantasy.

"I-I'm sorry. I . . . I scared you." Horror covered his dreadful-looking face with his twisted hands. "I'm so h-horrible," he moaned.

Fantasy pinched Horror's cheek. "You must never judge a book by its cover." When he heard this, Horror smiled his horrible smile.

"Look," said Fantasy, "he's smiling."

"That's a smile?" Richard sounded doubtful.

"All right! All right! Tea time's over!" Adventure was getting impatient. "Let's start navigatin' this here house."

Horror leapt out of Richard's arms and ran up to the house. Pressing up against the door, he blocked the way. "No! You can't go in there!"

"And why not?" asked Adventure.

"It's s-scary inside."

"Ha! I ain't afeard of nothin'." Adventure puffed out his chest and slashed his sword through the air.

Horror turned to Richard. "I-I'm a-afraid."

"Of what?" Richard was beginning to feel sympathetic toward this book. For once, somebody seemed to be just as afraid as he was.

Horror began to list his fears as he pointed, one by one, to his crooked, triple-jointed fingers. "I'm afraid of . . . the dark, dentists, butterflies, cucumbers . . ."

"Cucumbers?" That's one Richard hadn't thought of. "I know just how you feel," he said.

"Horror always has sad endings," Horror stated glumly as he twisted his foot and

rocked back and forth just like a kid.

Fantasy hugged Horror tightly. "Now, now," she reassured him, "I come from a world of happy endings. Why don't you come with us?"

"Yeah! I bet you know the best way through the house!" Richard was excited.

"Through the house?" Horror looked frightened.

"You can do it." Fantasy offered encouragement.

Horror hesitated. "Okay." He grabbed the doorknob, looking back at them for reassurance, then pushed the door in.

As the door opened, a sliver of light cut across the dark room. Rats scattered into the shadows. Horror entered cautiously, followed by Richard, Adventure, and Fantasy.

"He-hello? Anybody home?" Richard's voice filled the darkness.

"Nevermore!" A croaky voice came out of the darkness, and a huge black raven swooped down over their heads. Richard and Horror panicked. They made a grab for the doorknob, which fell off and rolled across the floor.

They watched the sparkling crystal knob roll slowly into the house. It stopped abruptly under the boot of a tall, silhouetted figure.

"May I assist you in some way?" asked the figure.

Adventure drew his sword, fearful that the

mysterious speaker might be an enemy.

But the figure stepped forward and turned up the flame on the gaslight fixture on the wall. The brighter light revealed a kind-looking, middle-aged man.

Fantasy primped her hair. "Oh, hello there, Mr. . . ."

"Doctor. Dr. Jekyll."

"Oh, you're a doctor." Fantasy was impressed. She twisted the bottom of her wand and out popped a lipstick. She quickly ran it over her lips.

"Well, sir," Richard started to explain, "we did ring the bell, but—"

"It's all my fault," Horror suddenly interrupted them. "I was trying to help them find

their way to the other side of the house."

"The other side?" The phrase seemed to disturb the good doctor. He laid a hand on Richard's shoulder and led him deeper into the house. "My boy, I derive no pleasure in telling you that you are in extreme danger."

"Danger?" That was one of Richard's least favourite words.

"Even as we speak, forces of evil are lurking in this very room, waiting to strike ."

"Evil?" Now Richard was really nervous.

"All human beings are possessed of both good and evil."

Richard looked suspiciously at his friends. They looked suspiciously at each other.

"But enough of that." Dr. Jekyll walked

over to a table covered with beakers and test tubes. There he opened up an apothecary cabinet filled with more laboratory equipment.

"Anyone care to join me for a drink?" The doctor poured a red liquid into a glass, and added a touch of powder. The mixture fizzed and threw off small plumes of vapour. The compound changed to a dark purple, then faded to a watery green.

Richard looked at the drink and shook his head, no.

"I'll have a go with ya', Doc!" Adventure licked his lips and smoothed his moustache with his hook.

The doctor plopped an olive into the drink and handed it to Richard, who handed it to Fantasy. She took a whiff. The smell made her eyeballs roll toward each other. She faked a smile, then turned to Adventure. "Sure seems like your kind of drink," she said, handing him the glass. Horror watched the exchange with drooling anticipation.

"Can I have the olive, please?" Horror begged shamelessly.

Adventure shoved Horror away. "Stand back! This is a man's drink!"

"Just the olive! That's all!" Horror yanked on Adventure's arm, and the watery green liquid flew into the air. Richard and his friends watched it travel across the room in a graceful arc. It landed with a splash on the floor.

"Now look what ye've done!" Adventure pointed at the spilled drink. It was beginning

to sizzle and burn its way through the hardwood floor.

Richard whipped around to warn Dr. Jekyll not to touch his drink, but he was too late. The doctor began to stagger around the room, screaming and clutching his throat. He was gasping for breath. Richard knew that in a situation like this you should call the poison hot line. He looked around for a phone. But he already knew that he wasn't likely to find one in a nineteenth-century haunted house.

The doctor's eyes turned a fiery red. He flung his glass into the fireplace, and the fire turned into a roaring inferno. Stumbling forward, he placed a hand on Richard's shoulder for support. Richard looked at the hand. It was changing, growing thick and hairy.

Richard tore loose from his grasp. The doctor collapsed on the floor, writhing in pain, and covered his face in agony.

"Dr. Jekyll? Are you all right?" Fantasy asked.

The doctor spun around the floor like an animal, then finally struggled up to his feet. Fantasy fluttered back in shock.

Now the doctor's face was wretched and wrinkled and mad with anger. "My name is Mr. Hyde!" he shouted. His eyes, which had once looked so kind, were glazed over with hate.

Richard's knees were knocking together. "I-I think we'll be going now," he said very politely.

"No one leaves this house alive!" With one brutal sweep of his cane, Mr. Hyde shattered the delicate glass instruments in his laboratory. Like a wolf toying with its dinner prey, he thwarted each and every attempt by Richard and his friends to escape. They were trapped.

Horror leapt onto the mantelpiece, then up to an iron chandelier. As Mr. Hyde advanced, a creaking noise sounded from above.

The chandelier that Horror was standing on dropped from the ceiling, pushing Mr. Hyde right into the hole that the powerful drink had made in the floor. But as he fell, he grabbed the chandelier chain. It held tight, breaking his fall. Mr. Hyde laughed a hideous-sounding laugh and started to climb back up.

Richard was too frightened to move.

"The stairs, matey!" ordered Adventure, pulling the boy along.

"Help, Master!"

Everyone turned around when they heard Horror's pitiful cry. The poor book was caught in the chandelier chain.

Horror looked like a poor trapped animal, begging for mercy. Richard wanted to help, but he was too scared to move. To his alarm the weight of Mr. Hyde was dragging the chandelier toward the hole in the floor.

"Don't leave me, Master!" Horror cried. "Sanctuary! Sanctuary!"

"You've got to help him!" Fantasy pleaded with Richard. When he didn't do anything, she flew back to help Horror herself.

Pulling her see-through wings over her eyes for safety, she ignited the end of her wand like a blowtorch and set to work cutting through the chain. She succeeded in freeing Horror just as Mr. Hyde's head poked up into the room.

The minute that Horror jumped off, the chandelier slid across the floor like a hockey puck and disappeared down the hole. "AHH-HHhhhhhhh!" Hyde roared in defeat.

"Let's get out of here!" Fantasy and Adventure led the way to the stairs.

Richard felt bad. He had proved to be useless. Horror moved over and tried to comfort him. "It's okay, Master. I'd-a been twice as scared as you." Gently Horror took Richard's hand and led him to the stairway.

One set of stairs led up; another went down to a lower floor. Adventure smoothed his moustache with his hook while he considered the options. Not having a clue, he turned to Horror. "Well, which way is it?"

"Uh . . . This way!" Horror pointed down. At the bottom of the stairs a blood-red glow began to pulsate. They heard what sounded like a loud, steady heartbeat. Horror immediately pointed in the opposite direction—up! He scrabbled up the stairs as fast as his crooked feet could climb.

The staircase seemed to twist and turn forever. The higher they climbed, the darker and scarier it got. After a while the stone walls began to turn into rows of books. Richard reached out to touch one, but his hand passed right through it!

"Where are we?" Richard didn't think he liked this new place.

Moans, groans, clanking chains—the sounds of a haunting filled the air. Ghostly book characters circled overhead—Jacob Marley, King Hamlet, Dracula. All the dead spirits of horror fiction flew by, then disappeared into thin air. Richard rushed up the stairs, brushing ghosts away as if they were cobwebs.

When he finally reached the top, he saw a long hallway with different-coloured doors on each side. They seemed to present an endless number of choices.

"Which door?" Richard asked desperately.

Horror looked confused. "The blue door? . . . No. The yellow door? . . . No. Eeny, meeny, miny, moe . . ." he said, pointing at each door in turn.

Adventure had had enough. "Outta my way!" he said, pushing Horror aside. He reached for a doorknob.

"No, not that one!" Horror screamed. But he was too late. Adventure had yanked open the white door.

Swoosh! A razor-sharp pendulum swung out from the room, nearly turning Adventure into a two-volume set. Adventure shut the door in a hurry!

Now it was Fantasy's turn. "Always trust a woman's intuition," she said, choosing the pink door. She peeked in. Out came a gruesome-looking hand. It grabbed her by the throat and dragged her in.

Richard, Horror, and Adventure hurried up to the door. They could hear from inside the sound of bloodcurdling screams and noises that sounded like limbs being ripped apart. Just as they couldn't stand any more, the door swung open. Fantasy fluttered out, primping her hair. She slammed the door shut with her behind and muttered, "What a lightweight!"

Horror decided to try the black door.

"Ahhhhhhhh!" He screamed and slammed the door shut, terrified.

"W-what is it?" Richard stammered.

"It's so dark in there," Horror whimpered. "No night-light."

"Get in there!" Adventure whipped open the door and pushed Horror in.

The room was dim and cold, and it reeked of formaldehyde. Richard recognised the smell from his biology class, where they had used the chemical stuff to preserve dead things.

In the middle of the room stood a table covered with ancient-looking laboratory equipment and jars filled with pickled body parts. Nearby a huge sheet covered a long stone slab.

"Up there." Fantasy pointed her wand in the direction of an overhead trapdoor. "That looks like the way out." A narrow stone staircase led up to the door. Unfortunately, the staircase was at the other end of the room. They would have to walk past the sheet-covered slab.

"Shhhhh." Fantasy raised her wand to her lips. Taking the lead, Adventure drew out his sword and clopped as quietly as he could past the slab. Horror and Richard were bringing up the rear. All at once they heard a low groan —"Arrgggghh."

Richard turned nervously to Horror. "I hope that was your stomach."

"I don't have a stomach," Horror replied.

"Arrrgggghh!" There came the scary groan again. Then the slab rotated forward. The sheet slithered down to the floor. Richard and Horror discovered that they were standing next to eight feet of stitched and rotting flesh.

"W-what's that?" Richard whispered.

Horror stood up on the tips of his toes to get a better look. "Um . . . it's either my Uncle Louie . . . or the Frankenstein monster."

"Frankenstein!" Richard shouted.

The monster's eyelids flew open. Its nostrils flared as it produced another horrible groan. "Arrrgggghhhh!"

Richard and Horror screamed, dashing for the stairs. But the monster lunged forward and grabbed Richard by the shirt. "Lemme goooo!" The boy struggled, but the monster was slowly dragging him back.

"The rope, lad! Look to the rope!" Adventure called down from the stairs. Richard looked up and discovered a rope that secured a hanging platform of electrical equipment high above the room. He jumped up and grabbed it.

Adventure cut the rope at the other end with his sword, and the platform plunged to the floor, shooting Richard up out of the monster's grasp.

"Arrrrgggggghhhh!" Frustrated and angry, the monster was thrashing back and forth.

Thanks to the rope, Richard was now up to the trapdoor, where he joined his friends. Together they pushed the trapdoor open and scrambled to an outside deck at the very top of the tower. A gargoyle statue held a torch that lighted up the stone wall encircling the deck. Beyond, there was nothing but darkness.

"This way, mateys!" Adventure jumped up onto the wall and started to climb down the other side. Horror followed right behind him.

Richard looked over the wall into a deep, dark unknown. "No way," he objected.

"Honey, you gotta go!" Fantasy flew over Richard on her way down.

In spite of his terrible fear, he finally decided to follow his friend. He was doing okay until one of the stones under his foot slipped. He managed to grab hold of a waterspout, but how long could he hang on?

The books watched Richard from a ledge

below. "Master needs help!" Horror was worried.

"Help ain't what that boy needs," Adventure countered.

"Oh, you're the expert," Fantasy said as she started to fly up to help Richard.

Adventure stopped her. "Leave 'im be. It's time he started findin' his own way."

Richard's arms were getting tired.

"The vine, boy! Grab the vine!" Adventure pointed with his sword toward the vine growing on the wall next to Richard. The boy reached out and grabbed it. But as soon as he let go of the waterspout, the vine snapped off the wall! Richard shut his eyes and swung down like Tarzan, letting out a much, much louder yell than Tarzan ever made.

Fortunately the vine deposited him safely onto the ledge right beside his friends. Examining himself for broken bones, Richard was amazed to find that he was all right. "Wow!" he exclaimed. He had made it by himself!

"Do ye smell it? Breathe it in, mates!" Adventure took a deep breath and pointed his sword out into the darkness. There, in the distance, the exit sign faintly glowed.

"The exit! The exit!" Horror cheered.

Just then, the sun began to rise, revealing a vast and beautiful ocean. It warmed the sandy tropical beach, the tall palm trees, and the high, jagged cliffs.

Adventure boldly thrust his chin out and raised his trusty sword. "There it be! The land of Adventure!"

Adventure

unlight illuminated the face of the cliffs, which seemed to be made entirely of books. Adventure led the way down a narrow, book-lined path toward the rocky shore below. Horror followed, shouting, "Hey! Wait for me!" ❦ Richard lagged behind. His descent was slow and careful. Clinging to the cliff side of the path, he carefully tested every step. Fantasy fluttered alongside him, offering words of advice and encouragement. ❦ Adventure had already reached the shore. He made his way to a huge rock jutting out over the water. "Ah! Home, sweet home!" he shouted. "Ain't it grand!" ❦ In his excitement, Horror tried to give Adventure a big hug. ❦ "Get yer hands off me!" Adventure twisted out of Horror's embrace. ❦ "Sorry," Horror uttered sadly, his lower lip quivering. ❦ Adventure turned back to the water and continued to admire the scene. Taking a deep breath, he slashed his sword triumphantly through the salty air. "Ain't nothing like the sea t' let a man know he's alive!"

EXIT

Suddenly, a huge wave lifted up before him and splashed down over his head. Horror started to laugh. Spinning around, Adventure aimed his sword right at Horror's heart.

"What're yer laughin' at, hunchbook?" he sputtered from under his wet moustache.

A starfish, swept up by the waves, had attached itself to Adventure's nose. Adventure rolled his eyeballs around, trying to see what was stuck to his face. Horror laughed so hard that he slipped on the wet rock. Scrambling wildly to stay upright, he grabbed Adventure's peg leg. They both slid off the side of the rock.

Richard and Fantasy were watching from the shore. "They fell in!" Richard exclaimed. Fantasy flew up over the rock. Richard followed. From the top of the rock, they looked down toward the water, expecting the worst.

Fortunately, Horror and Adventure had fallen into a small boat. Horror had landed on top of Adventure. "Hi, guys!" Horror was grinning happily.

"Will you just get off me!" Adventure wrestled out from under Horror. Suddenly he realised he was in a boat. He couldn't believe his luck. "A boat!" he shouted. "C'mon, ya lubbers! Climb aboard!"

Fantasy helped Richard into the old boat. Richard immediately asked, "Is it safe?"

"I've set to sea in worse," Adventure answered. "Ain't a craft afloat ever got the best of me!" He stamped his peg leg to prove his point. It went through the bottom of the boat.

When he jerked his peg out of the hole, a geyser of water shot up into Fantasy's bloomers.

"Ooooh, that's cold!" she shrieked.

Water started to fill the boat. Horror panicked. "We're sinking! We're going down! Somebody do something!"

Richard reacted quickly to the emergency. He pulled out his handkerchief and stuffed it into the hole. The water stopped gushing.

"Thank you." Horror smiled sweetly at Richard.

"You! And you!" Adventure pointed his sword at Richard and Horror. "Man the oars." Already he was taking command.

"And me?" Fantasy asked.

"You? You can just sit there quietly, missy. We're on to the land of Adventure now!" He jabbed his sword out toward the open sea. "Shove off, lads!"

The boat jumped the breakers as it plied its way toward the vast horizon. Richard was apprehensive. "The water looks pretty choppy. Maybe we should've stayed where it was safe."

Adventure turned to the frightened boy. "Lad, a ship in port may be safe." He smoothed out his moustache with his hook. "But that's not what ships were made fer."

The boat glided through a mysterious curtain of fog into the open sea. Puffs of purplish grey clouds dotted the blue sky like smoke signals warning of danger. In long, regular waves, the ocean began to swell and roll.

"Ships ahoy!" Adventure was the first to

spot four small boats ploughing over the swells off the starboard side. They were in perfect formation, a half-dozen men in each. "Whalin' men!" Adventure shouted with admiration.

Poised over the bow of the lead ship, a bearded, sinewy old man searched the water with wild eyes. He was wearing a ragged captain's coat, and had a peg like Adventure's in place of one of his legs.

"Look! Another guy with a peg leg!" Richard was amazed.

"Seems to be a fashion statement around here." Fantasy glanced sideways at Adventure.

"It's Captain Ahab, it is." Adventure grinned widely. "Straight out of *Moby-Dick*. Have you read it, boy? It's a whale of a book!"

Now the whalers were only metres away.

Ahab shouted toward Richard. "D'ye see him?"

"See who?" Richard shouted back.

Ahab didn't reply. His attention was on the water ahead. "Thar she blows!" Ahab thrust his knotted finger out toward the horizon.

All heads swivelled. Something very big was surfacing. The water parted and an enormous white whale exploded up through the surface!

"W-what's that?" Richard asked as he turned to Adventure.

"The devil of the deep, the white whale, Moby Dick!"

From the whale's blowhole a spray of water shot thirty metres into the air. Rivers of water cascaded down the giant whale's mountainous flank. Its small dark eyes blinked and focused on the whalers in their boats.

"I grin at thee, thou grinning whale!" Ahab laughed maniacally, ordering his fleet to head straight for the white whale. The whale had the same idea. He headed straight for Ahab on a deadly collision course.

"He's insane!" Fantasy pointed at Ahab.

"He's possessed!" Horror screamed.

"He's my kind of guy!" Adventure saluted.

Moby Dick thrust up out of the water, somehow lifting his whole body completely above the ocean surface.

It looks just like he's catching air, Richard thought.

"He's breaching!" a voice shouted.

Ahab readied his harpoon. "Thou damned whale! Thus I give up the spear!" Ahab hurled his deadly iron weapon into the solid white buttress of the whale's head.

Moby Dick smashed into the boats, ripping apart every last one. Men and timbers shot into the air. Ahab shouted no more.

Wreckage littered the water's surface as the white whale swam off. Richard and the books watched in terror as the whale began a sweeping arc. The monster of the deep was returning, approaching at incredible speed "H-he's coming for us now!" Richard screamed.

"Row! Row fer yer lives!" Adventure drew his sword and leapt atop the bow of the boat. Richard and Horror grabbed the oars and began pumping as fast as they could.

The whale caught the boat in its mouth, crushing it as it shot up toward the heavens.

"Abandon sh-i-i-ip!" Adventure shouted. But his order came too late. His friends were already tumbling into the thrashing water below.

Richard sank down, down into the water like a stone, passing pieces of wood and debris from the wreckage. His eyes were still wide open, but he was trying to hold his breath. Unexpectedly, something bumped him from below. It was a barrel rising to the surface. He grabbed hold and floated up toward the light.

The barrel shot up through the surface of the water. Scattered debris was bobbing in the water everywhere. There was nothing else—just Richard and the floating debris. Moby Dick had destroyed everything.

Richard looked around for the books. "Hey, guys? Where are you?" How could they just leave him like that? They were his friends. The only friends he'd ever had.

Then, not far from the barrel, something stirred the surface of the water. Richard panicked. He thought Moby Dick must be returning. Frantically he dog-paddled over to a raft-like plank and climbed aboard. But it was Adventure who surfaced, waterlogged and barely alive. "Adventure!" Richard pulled the listless book up onto the plank. Using his first aid training, Richard pumped Adventure's pages like a bellows. Water squirted out of the pirate book's mouth like a fountain.

The old seaman coughed and sputtered and slowly came around. Richard hugged him. "Boy, am I ever glad to see you!"

Adventure twisted out of the hug. "All right! All right! Enough with the huggin'!"

"Where're Horror and Fantasy?" Richard asked. Adventure looked away.

"I searched for 'em much as I could, mate. 'Fraid they've gone below with Davy Jones." Adventure sadly removed his bandanna.

"You mean they're . . . ?" Reality began to sink in. Richard slumped down onto the plank and began to cry.

"She's a cruel sea, my lad." Adventure offered his bandanna to Richard.

But Richard refused to believe they were really dead. He got to his feet, cupped his hands around his mouth and began to shout as loudly as he could.

"Horror! . . . Fantasy! . . ." Turning around to call in a different direction, he spotted a group of dorsal fins racing toward their plank. "Sharks!!!"

Adventure slashed his sword at the circling shark fins. "We may be seein' them other two sooner than ye think."

Then, from out of a mysterious veil of fog, a skiff appeared. "Look!" Richard began to wave his hands frantically over his head. "Help! Over here!"

Adventure squinted his good eye to get a better look. "Careful, mate. Not all sharks are in the water."

Two mangy sailors grinned as they man-oeuvred their skiff alongside the plank. They didn't look as if they had five teeth between them. Gum disease, Richard thought.

The taller sailor was dressed like a pirate, with dirty-looking clothes and a hefty flint-lock pistol stuffed into his thick belt. He pulled them on board.

"We're missing two others. Did you see 'em?" Richard asked.

"Yer all the catch we had t'day," the tall sailor said. The short sailor laughed and blew a ship's whistle. Another ship's whistle answered from inside the mysterious fog.

Richard looked up in awe. A huge Spanish galleon, in full sail, crashed through the veil of fog, almost burying the small skiff. The name, *Hispaniola*, was painted on its flank.

"I knew it! It's him!"" Adventure pointed up toward the top of the ship. Flying high over the mainmast was the infamous pirate flag, the Jolly Roger.

"It's *who*?" Richard was already worried enough.

"The meanest, most black-hearted pirate who ever sailed the seven seas." Adventure slowly reached for his sword.

But the tall sailor had already drawn out his flintlock. Brandishing it, he ordered, "Jest sit yer keel down, mate. John Silver's expectin' live company."

Richard was the first to come flying over the starboard rail of the *Hispaniola*. He hit the deck and tumbled to a stop in the middle of a bunch of filthy cutthroat pirates. Things were definitely not looking good!

A fat pirate named George Merry lifted Richard to his feet, waving a rusty knife in front of his face. Richard backed away from the knife into the arms of rotten-toothed Tom Morgan. Tom raised his cutlass up under Richard's chin. "Give the word, Cap'n Silver, sir, and I'll show ya the colour of his insides."

"Red! Red! My insides are red!" Richard shouted, hoping to convince the pirate that there was no need to open him up.

"Stow yer cutlass, Tom Morgan," came a deep voice from the stern. "I want a better look at his outsides first." A hulking, one-legged figure hobbled up in front of Richard. He was leaning against a crutch fashioned out of an old tree branch. Perched on his shoulder was a parrot, as mangy and mean as any of the pirates. Silver squinted down at Richard.

"Are you L-long John Silver?" Richard asked in amazement.

"Aye, lad. The very same. Right out of *Treasure Island*." Silver hobbled around Richard, squeezing the boy's tender shoulders with his huge calloused hand. "He's the runt of the litter all right. But he'll do."

"Do for what?" asked Richard.

"Well, seein' as how me men plucked ye out of the water like a drownin' bilge rat, you'll be joinin' our happy family as our new cabin boy." Silver gestured around the circle of dirty pirates.

Richard faked a smile. "Uh, thanks. But I already have a family. And I'm sure they're

wondering where I am. I think I'll just be getting home now."

The gang of pirates pointed their weapons at Richard. "Me men think ye are home." Silver grinned.

Suddenly there was a shout from the ship's rail. "John Silver! What do ye think yer doing?" There was Adventure, standing atop the deck rail. Adventure pointed a threatening finger at Silver. "Touch one hair on that boy's head and I'll chop yer liver so fine it won't be fit fer a party cracker!"

Silver grinned. "Come aboard, matey!" A pirate pushed Adventure down onto the deck in front of Silver.

"Well now, don't ye look familiar like." Silver spat and leaned in close to Adventure. "Ye wouldn't happen to be goin' after me treasure now, would ye?"

Adventure climbed to his feet and ruffled his pages. "Ye ain't got any treasure worth goin' after."

The other pirates, already distrustful of Silver, began to mutter uneasily among themselves. Silver reacted to the mutinous grumbling at once.

"He's lyin'," Silver shouted. "There's plenty of treasure fer all of ye!" Silver jabbed his crutch at Adventure. "Search 'im!" he ordered. "The boy, too."

Tom Morgan lifted Adventure and began to shake him upside down by his peg. An arsenal of late-eighteenth-century maritime weaponry poured out from between his pages. Flintlocks, knives, sabres, axes, and cannon-balls fell to the deck.

On the other side of Silver, George Merry was searching Richard. From one pocket he pulled out the nail and the five dollar bill his father had given him. From another, the library card. "Why lookee here, Cap'n." He handed the goods over to Silver.

Silver held up the five dollar bill. "Now what might this be?"

"It's money! You can keep it!" Richard said, hoping Silver could be bought off.

The pirates looked at each other and burst out laughing. Silver tossed the bill overboard.

Then he started picking his teeth with the nail as he turned his attention to the library card.

"That's my library card!" Richard protested. He didn't want to lose his passport out of this crazy place.

"A cabin boy don't need no library card." Silver tossed it overboard.

Richard and Adventure ran to the rail, watching the card flutter down toward the water. All hope of escape was vanishing with it.

In the sky behind Richard, clouds began to swirl and form themselves into a strange shape. It was the Pagemaster! With a mighty blast of wind, this cloudlike Pagemaster suddenly blew the library card across the surface of the ocean toward . . .

"Land ho!" A pirate in the crow's-nest shouted. Silver and his men rushed to the rail. Clearly

visible on the horizon was an island distinguished by a rocky cliff shaped like a skull.

"There she be, mateys." Silver jabbed his crutch out toward the skull. "Skeleton Island."

The parrot ruffled its wings. "Pieces of eight. Awk! Pieces of eight!"

Skeleton Island. Excited by the thought of buried treasure, the pirates hurried up the sandy shore after beaching their skiffs.

Silver hobbled along on his crutch. He cursed like a madman whenever flies settled on his sweaty flesh. Tugging at the rope holding Richard and Adventure captive, he would occasionally fix them with a deadly stare.

Adventure spoke under his breath to Richard. "Stay on yer toes, mate. Soon as Silver goes for the gold, we'll make our break."

A group of pirates stopped dead in their tracks next to the remains of a human skeleton. The bony, dry skeleton lay perfectly straight. Its feet pointed in one direction; its arms and hands, raised above its head, were pointing in the direct opposite direction.

"W-what sort of way is that for bones t' lie?" asked one of the pirates. "'Tain't natural." Richard couldn't help noticing that as mean and ruthless as pirates were, they also seemed to be a superstitious lot, deathly afraid of spirits.

"This island's haunted," said a second pirate. "It's accursed, it is!"

Silver examined the skeleton. "Ye yellow sea dogs! The bones is the compass pointin' the way to the doubloons!"

The pirates broke into a run toward the treasure, but then they stopped abruptly. Something was wrong. Silver hobbled up. Before him was a deep pit. At the bottom rested an open, clearly empty treasure chest.

"It's gone! The treasure's gone!" George Merry jumped into the pit, dropping to his knees. He raked the sand with his fingers, but came up with only a single gold piece. "One gold piece!" He lifted the coin defiantly before Silver. "This your treasure, is it?"

Adventure turned to Richard. "Stand by for trouble."

"We might have known you'd double-cross us!" Merry turned to the other men, who who started to grumble in agreement.

Silver reached for his flintlock, but the other pirates beat him to it. A dozen guns, swords, and knives were pointed directly at him.

"Throw down yer weapon, John Silver." Merry ordered.

"You'll be regrettin' this, George Merry." Silver reluctantly tossed down his flintlock.

"Save yer speeches." Merry gestured for the pirates to take aim. "Dead men don't bite."

Richard shut his eyes tight and swallowed hard. Adventure did the same.

"Aaaaahh-oooooooo!" A horrible, ghostly howl descended from the trees. The pirates' heads swerved upward. Their faces shared the same terrified look. "W-what w-was that?"

The ghostly voice then continued loudly, "Fifteen men on the dead man's chest. Yo-ho-

ho and a bottle of ruuuuuummmmm!"

"E-evil spirits!" Tom Morgan cried.

Another voice, higher pitched but just as spooky, joined the first. "Aaa-ooooo! Your mama drinks bilge water."

The pirates moved their flintlocks around, trying to track the voices.

"Oooo-ver here!" The first voice wailed.

"Nooo. Over here, stupid." The higher voice returned.

The pirates frantically glanced from tree to tree. There was a rustle of leaves, then something swung down over the pirates' heads. Bang! Bang! Bang! Bang! Pistol balls flew in every direction.

"Sanctuary! Sanctuary!"

Richard felt a surge of joy at the familiar voice. "Horror! You're still alive!"

"Not for long!" George Merry was aiming his flintlock directly at Horror.

"Weeeeeeeee!" Something swung down past Merry's face, leaving a trail of pixie dust in its wake.

"Fantasy!" Richard shouted.

Merry tried to hold back a sneeze. "Ah-ah-ah-chooooo!" His flintlock went off, blasting a cluster of coconuts off a tree. They fell on Tom Morgan's head, knocking him out cold.

George Merry was spitting mad. "Get them!" he shouted. In the scramble that followed, Silver's crutch was knocked out from under him. He cursed and grunted as he dragged himself over the sand to retrieve it.

Adventure was grinning. Finally there was going to be a good fight. He lifted his sword and slashed at the rope that bound him to Richard. The snap of the rope sent him reeling. He fell backwards over the edge of the pit and into the treasure chest. Horror, who was escaping from a pirate, jumped on top of the chest, accidentally slamming it shut.

"Lemme outta here! Lemme outta here!" Adventure cried. But his muffled shout went unanswered.

The fight continued. Two pirates attacked Fantasy, swiping at her with their cutlasses. Swiftly she flew above them and tied their pigtails together. They chased after her but their pigtails soon snagged on a tree, causing them to whip around and smash into each other. Down they went.

Nearby, Horror was circling round and round another pirate, getting him so dizzy that he was soon seeing double. Two Horrors, then quadruple Horrors, then hundreds of Horrors were surrounding him. Horror made his most monstrous face, shouting "Booga-booga-booga!"

The pirate screamed in terror and ran off.

Silver was climbing to his feet when the terrified pirate ran past, bumping against him. Silver stumbled forward only to find himself face to face with Richard. Now it was pirate against boy. On the ground, midway between them, lay a cutlass. They both saw it at the same time.

Richard stared straight into Long John Silver's squinting, watery, eyes. The pirate was more than twice the boy's size. Normally Richard would have run, but for once his heart —beating fast and sure—was telling him to stand his ground.

Fantasy fluttered up behind Richard. "The sword, honey," she whispered. "Go for the sword."

Silver's gaze shifted from Richard to the cutlass, then back to Richard. "Don't even think of it, boy! Ye ain't got the heart." Silver made the first move. But Richard was quicker.

"S-s-stay back," the boy ordered as he lifted the heavy cutlass in his small hands and aimed it directly toward Silver's big gut. Silver squinted, his eyes darting back and forth between Richard and the razor-sharp cutlass. "Avast, lad. Somebody could get hurt with that blade ye got there."

"I-I know." Richard had to agree. "Twenty-three percent of all injuries are caused by knives or other sharp objects."

"What . . . ?" This statement caught Silver off guard for a second. "Er . . . right ye are, boy."

Silver glanced over Richard's shoulder at a beached skiff. Pointing to the small boat, he pleaded. "Yer not gonna make me get on that thar ship and row away now, are ye?"

Richard glanced at the skiff. "That's exactly what I'm gonna do!" he answered, wishing he had thought of the idea himself.

Richard moved backward to let Silver pass. Carefully, without taking his eyes off the cutlass, Silver hobbled down to the skiff. "Easy now, matey. Easy. I'm goin' peacefully. Right ye are, into the boat. Aye, aye!" Silver climbed into the boat and used his crutch to push off.

"Ye be a hard lad, Richard Tyler," Silver shouted. "Good sailin' to ye." His huge hands grabbed the oars. With a few sure strokes, the skiff was heading out to the open sea.

Richard glanced down at the cutlass. Suddenly his hands began to shake. The weapon fell to the sand. So did Richard. Fantasy and Horror rushed up, congratulating him on his bravery.

Richard was in shock. He couldn't believe what he had just done. "Boy, I wish my dad coulda seen me! . . . By the way, what happened to Adventure?"

A loud pounding noise came from inside the treasure chest. Horror scampered over. "Who's there?" he asked.

"It's me—Adventure!" came the muffled answer.

"Adventure who?" Horror liked riddles.

"Whaddaya mean, Adventure who? Open the blasted top of this coffin, you dog-eared . . ."

Horror raised the lid, and Adventure bounded out, swinging his sword, ready for a fight. "Let me at 'em!" he cried. Then he looked around and discovered that there was no one left to fight.

"You've got perfect timing, Robin Hood." Fantasy teased.

Adventure snarled and kicked at the sand.

Gesturing toward Fantasy and Horror, Richard said, "I was just thankin' these guys for savin' us."

"That was nothing," Adventure bragged. "I could've taken the lot of them with one hand tied behind me back!" Waving his hook in the air, he stomped off down the beach.

Horror picked up a bandanna lying on the sand and hobbled off after him.

Adventure was still moving down the beach, kicking sand and grumbling to himself, when Horror caught up to him.

"Ahoy, matey!" Horror had tied the bandanna over his head. In his hand he was swinging a piece of driftwood as if it was a pirate's sword. "Aye, we're lusty adventurous men!"

Adventure glared over at Horror. "Go away! Ye don't know what yer talkin' about!"

"I . . . I know I'm not your favourite kind of book. But I could be just like you." Horror smiled.

"You'll never be Adventure! Ye ain't got the spine fer it." Adventure pointed at Horror's bandanna. "And take that stupid thing off!"

Horror's lower lip began to tremble, as he pulled off the bandanna. "S-sorry."

Adventure walked off grumbling, leaving Horror feeling alone and rejected. In a few minutes Horror hobbled off down the beach in the opposite direction, not paying much attention to where he was going.

Richard was sitting next to the water. He had written the word EXIT on the sand with a stick. But a small wave soon slid up and washed the word away. He sighed.

"Why the long face? You were a real hero." Fantasy fluttered down in front of Richard.

"I lost my library card. Now I can't check you out. I can't check anybody out. We'll never get to the exit now." Richard rested his head on his knees.

Gently Fantasy raised Richard's chin up with her wand. "Never say never around Fantasy, honey. Sometimes you've got to fight to make a wish come true."

Farther down the beach, Adventure was still grumbling and kicking his way through the sand when a wet piece of paper stuck to his peg. He tried to shake it loose, but it wouldn't come off. Then he tried jumping up and down, but the paper still didn't budge. Finally, he sat down on the sand and peeled it off. His eyes opened wide when he realized what he was holding. He hurried back to where Richard and Fantasy were sitting.

"Why're ye sitting around like a bunch a old wenches at tea time?" he asked. Extending both his hand and his hook toward Richard, he said, "Pick one."

Richard considered his choices. "Mmm . . . that one." Richard picked Adventure's hand.

"Yer a bright lad," Adventure said, opening his fist.

"My library card!" Richard's face lighted up. "Where'd you find it?"

Adventure thumped his chest. "Why, I wrestled it away from three sharks who was eyein' it fer breakfast."

"Uh-huh. And Rapunzel wears a wig," Fantasy said, rolling her eyes in disbelief.

"Where's Horror?" Richard asked. "Wasn't he with you?"

Adventure scratched his head with his hook. "Well, he was . . . but he . . . I mean I sort of . . . he kinda . . . "

"Now what did you say to him!" scolded Fantasy.

"Well, I . . . uh . . . just . . . I'll go find him." Adventure plodded off down the beach calling, "Horrrr-or!"

Adventure climbed to the top of a tall sand dune and gasped in amazement. On the other side of the dune, the walls and towers of a tiny

storybook castle rose above the sandy beach. Outside the castle walls, scores of tiny fifteen-centimetre men were busy tying a lifeless-looking Horror to the ground with a series of ropes. They looked like the little Lilliputians from *Gulliver's Travels*.

Adventure drew his sword. Waving it over his head, he shouted. "Hang on, mate! Adventure's comin'!"

When they heard his thunderous voice, the Lilliputians quickly gathered in military formations and shot little arrows at Adventure. *"Tolgo phonac!"* they shouted.

Adventure flipped open his heavy binding like a shield, deflecting the little arrows, but one of them sank into his peg leg. Adventure bent over and yanked it out. "Say yer prayers, ye little two-legged shrimps!"

Breaking the arrow over his knee, Adventure charged straight at the tiny men.

The Lilliputian troops panicked, retreating in confusion into the brush.

"Come back, ye cowardly lubbers!" Adventure slashed his sword through the air triumphantly. "Ya ha! Did ye see 'em run, mate?" Horror didn't answer. Horror wasn't even moving. Quickly Adventure cut through the ropes with his sword. Lifting Horror's lifeless head,

he pleaded, "Speak t' me, matey! Ye had a good heart, ye did. And ye was braver than ye knew. I'd walk the plank if I thought it would bring ye back."

"You would?" Horror suddenly spoke. Adventure's eyes opened wide as saucers. He thrust Horror out in front of him. Horror was smiling his best horrible smile.

By this time, Fantasy and Richard had appeared on the scene.

"Aren't they just too cute!" Fantasy commented.

Adventure dropped Horror like a hot potato. Drawing his sword, he slashed it through the air in a manly fashion.

Richard rushed up to Horror. "Are you okay?"

"Thanks to my friend here, I am." Horror hugged Adventure.

"Never, never, never hug me again!" Adventure yelled.

Horror backed off. "O-okay."

"Did you see that?" Fantasy was staring at her wand.

"See what?" Richard looked at the wand. It blinked "on" for a millisecond.

"My wand. It's blinking! That can only mean one thing!" Fantasy was ecstatic.

"The exit?" Richard was still hopeful.

"The checkout desk?" Adventure was hopeful, too.

"A happy ending!" Horror started to jump up and down, clapping for joy.

Fantasy

sing Fantasy's blinking wand as a guide, Adventure bushwhacked a path through a dense tropical jungle that led away from the beach. They were passing through some kind of corridor, but no one knew where it led. Fantasy studied her flickering wand. "Are you sure that yard stick a yers is workin'?" Adventure asked impatiently. "Well, why don't we just test it and find out." Fantasy flicked the wand at Adventure. POOF! When the smoke had cleared, Adventure was floating in the air, dressed in fairy clothes—tutu, ballet slippers, wings, and lipstick. He looked at himself. "Ye've gone overboard this time, sister!" Adventure snarled. Fantasy studied the results of her magic. "You certainly are one ugly fairy," she said. Adventure shredded the costume with his sword, mumbling threats and other unmentionable things under his breath. As they moved farther into the jungle, the colours began to change. Many new and more brilliant hues fanned out before them.

EXIT

The spectacle filled Richard with awe. He was eager to see more. He pushed through a flower-lined thicket into a magical meadow. Fairy dust shimmered everywhere. Groves of trees hung heavy with fat, juicy buds. As Richard walked past, the ripe buds unfolded, offering not flowers, but books.

"Wow. Look at this place." Richard was mesmerised. Tiny Thumbelina flew over their heads on the back of a bird. She passed a castle tower where a handsome prince was climbing up the golden braid of his true love's hair. A majestic horse and carriage sped past. In a puff of light the carriage magically turned into a pumpkin and the horses into mice. The cheery little mice bounced around Adventure's feet, offering squeaks of friendship.

"Arrrrr!" Adventure grumbled with disgust. "Happyland."

The mice scampered toward Horror, who accepted them enthusiastically. He fell back onto a soft bed of giggling flowers, ready to burst with joy. "I could be misshelved here for a long time," he said.

Soon, whole clusters of shimmering fairies arrived. They danced through the air around Richard and the books.

"Hello, my little dearies." Fantasy greeted her twittering little friends.

An especially delicate fairy flew down and landed on Richard's open hand. He gazed happily into its warm glow. In a playful gesture, the fairy snatched Richard's glasses. Richard

laughed and gave chase. "Hey! My glasses!"

Adventure drew his sword. "I knew it! They're all little thieves!" A cluster of fairies descended over Adventure and made off with his sword. "Hey, now they've got my sword!"

"Oh, they're just being playful." Fantasy defended her friends.

"Playful! I'll show 'em playful when I get hold of the little . . ." Adventure clopped off after the fairies, yelling, "Come back here with my sword!"

The fairy with Richard's glasses flew up to the top of a rocky hill. Richard, laughing at the joke, chased up the hill after her.

The fairies with Adventure's sword entered a mysterious cave at the base of the hill. Adventure, Fantasy, and Horror all looked into the cave, wondering what they would find there. Adventure even lifted his eyepatch, hoping he might spot his sword. Inside the cave, a strong wind whipped ribbons of red smoke around rows of sharply pointed stalactites and stalagmites.

"It looks s-s-scary in there," Horror stammered.

"Well, what are you waiting for, an invitation? Is Adventure scared to go in?" Fantasy gave the old seaman a mocking glance. She was sure that he was stalling.

"Are you kiddin', sister? I live for moments like this!" Adventure reached for his sword, then remembered that it wasn't there. He felt naked without it. Clearing his throat, he led the way into the mysterious cavern with Fantasy and Horror following timidly behind him.

Back on the rocky mound above the cave,

Richard had taken his glasses back from the mischievous fairy. When he put them on, he noticed an amazing mountain in the distance. It seemed to be made entirely of books. A radiant light crowned its peak.

"Geez, there it is!" he exclaimed. Shimmering high above the mountain top was the exit sign.

Cautiously Adventure moved deeper into the hot, sticky cave. He found his sword there, lying on a stone. He grasped it firmly and held it up with obvious satisfaction. "Aye, it's good to have ye back, mate." He slashed it through the air, whacking off one of the stalactites, which dropped down and stuck into the soft cave floor. Suddenly the whole ground began to tremble and shake violently!

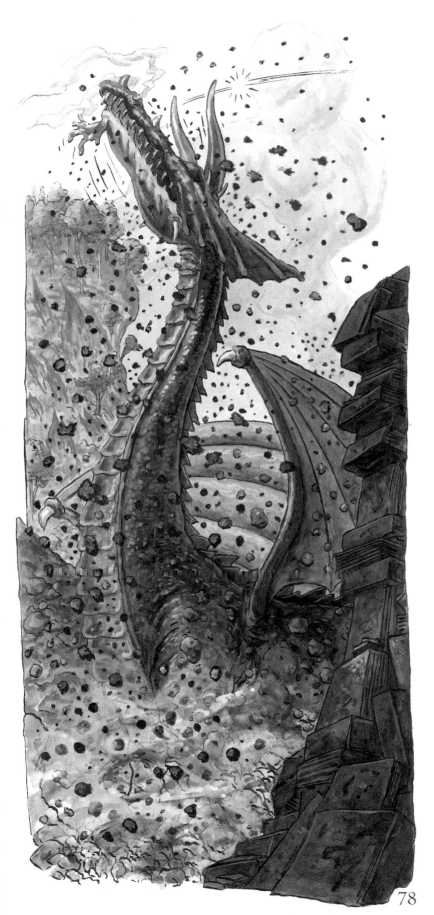

Meanwhile, up above, the rocks under Richard started to pitch and roll. His worst fear had come back to haunt him. "Earth-quaaaaake!" he shouted. He stumbled over to a broken, ivory-coloured tree trunk and held on for dear life. In front of him, two huge round rocks rolled upward, revealing a pair of red-hot eyes!

Suddenly Richard realised that he was not standing on top of a rocky hill at all. He was right on the nose of a terrible dragon! And his friends were not in a rocky cave. They were inside the dragon's mouth! The huge stalag-mites and stalactites were really the dragon's teeth. Adventure rushed at full speed toward the opening. A fireball shot out over his head just as he jumped out, with Fantasy and Horror right behind him.

As the dragon reared its ugly head, it shook centuries of rocks and earth off its gigantic frame. And its roar echoed across the land. Birds took flight. So did the wild animals. Richard's companions had awakened the sleep-ing dragon, and now somebody had to pay!

"Not to worry. I can handle this." Fantasy blew warm breath onto her blinking wand. "Don't fail me now," she said. She flicked the wand in the direction of the dragon. A few sparks ignited at the tip, then the wand went limp as a wet noodle. Fantasy shook her head. "Last time I buy a rechargeable wand."

All this time, the dragon was torching every-thing around it. Its huge leathery wings pumped vigorously, fanning the flames. The once beautiful meadow was now turning into a blazing inferno.

All at once, the dragon jerked its head back, throwing Richard high into the sky. He let out a bloodcurdling scream.

Fantasy turned to Horror. "Quick! Open me up. Find page one thousand and one!"

Horror licked his thumb and began slowly flipping through the pages. "Page one, page two, page three . . ."

"Faster! Faster!" Fantasy screamed.

Horror flipped through the pages at blinding speed. ". . . nine hundred ninety-nine, one thousand, one thousand and one . . . *Arabian Nights*?"

"That's it!" Fantasy ripped out the page. Snapping it out like a wet towel, she turned it into a flying carpet. "Save the boy!" she commanded the carpet. It took off instantly, dipping and swerving around the dragon. Just in time it found its way under Richard, who was about to hit the ground. Richard rode off on top of it.

The dragon shot a fireball at the carpet, which manoeuvred like a jet fighter plane, dodging the flame. Richard screamed as the carpet headed straight for a tree, but at the last second it swerved, then cut back, dipped down, and skidded to a stop next to the books.

Richard pointed up to the top of the moun-tain. "The exit's up there!" he said. "Quick, jump on the carpet." The books jumped on. But just as they were about to take off, the dragon's tail slammed down onto the carpet's edge, pinning it to the ground.

The jolt caused Fantasy's wand to pop on. This time its light was strong and steady. "Well, it's about time," she said. She flicked the wand toward the dragon. An electrified charge shot out of the tip of her wand and blasted the beast!

The angry dragon stopped in its tracks. A perplexed look crossed its face. Its eyes spun around like bingo balls. Then, in a fantastic explosion of smoke and sparks, it shrank into a harmless toad.

"Wow! How'd you do that?" Richard was amazed.

Fantasy proudly twirled the wand in her hand. "Magic."

"Women," Adventure grumbled under his breath. "Everything's magic to them."

The dragon-toad began to croak. Its eyes bulged out and its tail expanded by at least a metre. "Did I mention how fast a spell wears off on a dragon this size?" Fantasy said. The toad croaked again and grew six more metres! It blasted a spear of fire at the carpet, which shot off into the sky. Richard and the books clutched the carpet tightly as they streaked up into the clouds. It glided smoothly over the clouds. Though Richard was usually terrified

of heights, the ride excited him. He almost didn't want it to end.

Suddenly the carpet veered and swooped down lower, taking them over magical cloud worlds filled with giants, genies, and castles.

Then the carpet began to glide upward again toward the top of the mountain. "We're gonna make it!" Richard cheered.

"We're gonna make it!" Horror repeated. But he was so excited that he accidentally knocked Fantasy's wand out of her hand. It tumbled over the edge of the carpet.

"Ooops! I wish that hadn't happened." Fantasy leaned over to see where the wand would land. It fell right into the mouth of

the dragon, which was flying directly up toward them, flapping its enormous wings. Suddenly it shot a fireball. The fireball exploded before it reached them, but the impact was strong enough to knock the carpet out of control.

"What do we do now?!" Adventure asked Fantasy.

Fantasy lowered her head between her knees. "Assume crash positions, everyone!"

With a tremendous bump, the carpet crashed smack into the side of the mountain. Richard landed on his back on a ledge formed by books. He was looking straight up at the exit sign. It seemed almost close enough to touch.

Scrambling to his feet, he shouted, "C'mon, guys!"

The books, however, were tangled up in a heap below.

"Get off me!" Adventure struggled to get out from under Horror.

Fantasy fluttered up out of the pile, yanking on her bloomers. While their pages were rustling, a dark shadow passed over. The three books looked up into the sky. The dragon was about to land on them! They scrambled into a narrow crevice on the side of the book mountain. The dragon landed on the ledge, trapping them inside.

Meanwhile Richard was scrambling up the mountainside. In his excitement at reaching the exit, he hadn't even looked back. He thought the books were right behind him. "We're almost there!" he shouted. With a final burst of energy, he climbed up the last few metres and stepped triumphantly onto the mountain top. He could see the exit sign hovering over an ancient, dome-shaped observatory. He breathed a well-deserved sigh of relief.

"We did it, guys. We did it!"

Then Richard turned around and discovered he was all alone. Looking down the side of the mountain, he spied the dragon peering into the crevice.

Inside the crevice the books were nervously

looking out at the dragon, who reared back and shot a blast of flame at them. They flattened themselves against the wall so that the fire shot past.

"A man can only take so much." Adventure drew his sword. "This dragon is soon gonna be history!" He started toward the opening.

"Be careful," Fantasy said.

In a grand gesture, Adventure grabbed Fantasy and gave her one big juicy kiss. Her eyes opened wide in surprise.

"Hey! What do you think you're doing?" She gave Adventure a shove, and he tumbled out of the crevice.

From up above, Richard saw Adventure land on a ledge.

"Adventure, I'm up here!" he shouted. Adventure looked up and saw Richard calling to him from the top of the mountain.

"Go on lad! Save yerself!" Adventure shouted. Just then the dragon blasted another spear of fire in the old seaman's direction. Adventure stumbled back into the crevice, smoldering. His bandanna was burned, and the hairs of his big moustache were sizzling.

Horror blew out the flames.

Now Richard was caught in a real dilemma. He had made it all the way to the exit. He was almost free. The old Richard would have got out of there while he still had the chance. No question about it. But what about his new friends? Could he just abandon them? Weren't these books important enough for him to risk

his ten-year-old neck trying to save them?

"Help, Master!" Richard heard Horror's distant wail coming up from below. "Sanctuary! Sanctuary!"

Richard closed his eyes, and made the toughest decision he had ever had to make. "Hang on, guys!" he shouted, racing down the side of the mountain. He stopped just long enough to borrow a sword, shield, and helmet from a knight's skeleton that lay alongside the path.

Lifting the sword into the air, he yelled, "I'm coming!"

Richard bounded down the mountain until he and the dragon stood face to face. Though terrified, the boy held his ground, slashing away with his sword. The dragon shot another spear of fire out of its mouth. It exploded against Richard's shield!

The books peeked out from the crevice.

"That's it, boy! Go fer the gizzard!" Adventure shouted, slashing his sword through the air.

"Watch out for his tail!" Fantasy was nervously twisting Adventure's bandanna.

"Bite 'im! Bite 'im!" Horror jumped up and down.

Richard aimed his sword toward the dragon's soft spot, under the lower part of its neck. But before he could strike, the dragon whipped its tail around and snared the boy. His sword and shield fell to the ground as the powerful tail lifted him into the air.

"Put me down, you ugly . . . " But before Richard could finish his sentence, the dragon,

in one large gulp, had swallowed him whole.

Adventure, Fantasy, and Horror stared at each other in disbelief. "What a sad, sad ending," Fantasy whispered.

"Master wasn't afraid of nuthin'," Horror cried. "Aye, a braver lad never sailed the seven seas," Adventure agreed.

Sadly, Horror turned to grasp Adventure, but stopped. Adventure hesitated, then reached for the hunchbook. Fantasy joined the huddle.

Richard had tumbled down through the long throat tunnel onto the pillowy bottom of the stomach. He quickly discovered that the in-

side of the dragon's stomach was a pulsating slime pit. The cavity was littered with bones, piles of books, trees and anything else a dragon might eat. Loud grumbling noises were followed by small, random eruptions of fire.

There Richard found Fantasy's wand. He tried to make it work, but it refused to respond. This is not good at all, he thought.

Up above, a pinpoint of light filtered down through the dragon's throat. Richard realised that up there was his only possible means of escape. He climbed on top of a stack of books and reached up as high as he could. But the

books slipped and toppled, sending him back to the bottom of the dragon's stomach.

Frustrated, Richard began to kick at the books. Then he remembered something the Pagemaster had said: "When in doubt, look to the books."

Richard opened an old copy of *Alice in Wonderland*. Like a jack-in-the-box, the crazy Queen of Hearts's head popped out, hysterically ranting: "Off with his head! Off with his head!"

Richard slammed the book shut and the Queen was gone. Then he got another idea. He began searching frantically through the piles of books, rejecting one after another. Suddenly he found what he was looking for —*Jack and the Beanstalk*. Opening the book, he placed it on the bottom of the dragon's stomach. At first nothing. Then the book began to shake and rumble. Richard stepped back in anticipation.

A thick beanstalk started to shoot up out of the pages! The stalk grew faster and faster, coiling up through the dragon's throat.

Richard leapt onto the stalk and shot up with it. "I hate heeiigghhttss!"

The dragon's eyes opened wide. His head jerked back, and his mouth flipped open. Suddenly, out shot the giant beanstalk!

Adventure, Fantasy, and Horror watched in amazement. They were even more surprised when Richard came riding up out of the dragon's mouth.

"C'mon!" Richard yelled. "Jump on." He gathered the books in his arms and up they all went. They jumped off at the top of the mountain.

Horror hugged Richard's legs. "Master, you saved us!"

"That ye did, matey."

"You did good, honey," said Fantasy. When she saw that he was carrying her wand in his pocket, she kissed him on the cheek. "My hero," she gushed.

Richard looked up. Just ahead of them, hovering over the observatory, he saw the glowing green exit sign.

The tall oak doors pushed open. Richard and the books entered a circular room. Their faces were illuminated by a bright funnel of light rising up out of a gigantic crystal dome.

Something shifted in the shadows. "Who's there?" Richard strained for a better look. Slowly, a figure stepped out into the light.

"My Pagemaster." Adventure removed his bandanna and bowed respectfully. Horror threw himself onto the floor. Fantasy curtsied.

"Hey! How did you get here!" Richard was not too pleased to see the Pagemaster again.

"Now, now. We're in the presence of the Pagemaster." Fantasy laid a hand on Richard's shoulder, trying to silence him.

"I know who he is. He's the guy who put me through all that torture! Just look at me," Richard said, calling attention to his dirty and tattered, clothing. "Do you have any idea what I've been through?"

"Tell me." The Pagemaster seemed interested.

Richard collected his thoughts. "Well . . . I was nearly torn apart by a mad doctor. I was made a slave by a bunch of mangy pirates. And, believe it or not, I was even eaten by a fire-breathing dragon. Not to mention being tossed, squashed, and scared practically to death!"

"Yet you stand before me." The Pagemaster's steady gaze gradually overcame Richard's stubborn resistance.

"Well . . . yeah."

Horror knelt at the Pagemaster's feet, begging mercy for his disrespectful friend. "He don't mean nuthin' by it, my Pagemaster. He don't mean it."

"Nonsense! The boy is right. I purposely sent him through the fiction section."

"So you admit it?" Richard felt vindicated.

"Of course! . . . Think, boy! What kind of an adventure would you have had if I'd brought you here with a turn of the page?" He waved his staff over the crystal dome. The light in it began to waver. A ghostly image of Mr. Hyde appeared inside the funnel, then quickly changed into the gentle Dr. Jekyll, who tipped his hat to Richard. "You prevailed over evil."

Other images appeared inside the funnel —Captain Ahab and Long John Silver. Ahab pointed his finger at Richard. "Ye looked Moby Dick in the eye, boy!"

Long John Silver looked at Richard and gave him a wink. "Ye had true pirate stuff, m'lad." He placed his big hand over his cutlass. "And

don't ye let no one speak any different."

Now the Pagemaster pointed his staff at Richard. "If I had brought you here from the start you never would have found the courage to face your own fears."

Richard gasped as the dragon materialised inside the funnel. It blasted a spear of fire mist, then faded away with the other images.

"And in doing so you triumphed and will always triumph."

Richard felt good. Proud. Almost invincible. Fantasy cast a halo of fairy dust over his head.

With a wave of the Pagemaster's staff, the crystal dome glowed brightly. Richard gazed into the glass. He was looking down into the library rotunda, where his body lay motionless on the floor. "Hey, that's me!"

"That was you," said the Pagemaster.

"I'm ready to go back now—I mean, we're ready." Richard gathered Adventure, Fantasy, and Horror around him.

"Your world awaits." The Pagemaster waved his staff. A whirlwind suddenly whipped up above the dome, sweeping Richard and the books into its vortex of swirling light.

The sound was deafening—a cacophonous mix of wind, fluttering pages, and murmuring voices. The voices were whispering phrases that now had meaning for Richard: "Fiction from A to Z, where all is possible," "It's the devil of the deep, the white whale!" "All human beings are possessed of both good and evil," "He's the meanest, most black-hearted

pirate who ever sailed the seven seas," "Sanctuary! Sanctuary!" "And they all lived happily ever after. . . ."

The mural at the top of the rotunda became a swirling blur. A column of bright colours dipped down from the centre, taking Richard and the books with it.

Richard fell straight down into his prostrate body. Next to him, Adventure, Fantasy, and Horror, all hit the hard marble floor—Slam! Slam! Slam!—and turned into ordinary books.

Richard's eyes opened wide. He was staring up at the mural. His gaze was fixed on the painted image of the Pagemaster. Then, out of nowhere, the librarian, Mr. Dewey, was leaning over Richard, blocking the Pagemaster's image. "You took quite a spill, young man."

"Huh?" Richard shook his head, trying to think more clearly. He looked around. Above the stacks, he saw the exit sign, looking as if it had always been there. Without thinking, without any hesitation, he scrambled to his feet and ran toward it.

"Careful, or you'll slip again." Mr. Dewey warned him. He began collecting the three old dusty books off the floor.

Down the aisle, Richard skidded to a stop. He looked back and saw Mr. Dewey gathering the books. "Wait!" he called.

Richard ran back into the rotunda. "I forgot something." He took the books out of Mr. Dewey's arms and presented his library card.

Mr. Dewey examined the torn and dirty card with interest. "I'm afraid you can only check out two today," he said, removing Horror from the top of the stack.

"But I promised I'd check him out."

"You promised whom?"

Richard pointed to Horror. "Him . . . I mean . . . umm. . . . Do you think just this once I could? . . . Please, Mr. Dewey, I really need . . ."

Mr. Dewey raised a silencing hand. "Shhh. I have a talent for guessing what people need." He glanced around to make sure that no one was watching, then placed Horror back in Richard's arms. "Just this once."

Richard thanked Mr. Dewey and hurried down the aisle toward the exit.

"Godspeed to you, boy!"

The rain-washed streets glimmered with the orange light of the setting sun. The storm had passed. Richard rode his bike with confidence down the tree-lined street. The three books were nestled comfortably in the bicycle basket.

Richard turned a corner. Dead ahead, the bike-riding kids were still gathered around the ramp. Richard stopped.

"Look who came back!" one of the kids called.

"Hey, Tyler, ya gonna chicken out again?"

Richard's heart pumped fast but sure as he steered his bike toward the ramp. The bike picked up speed. Faster and faster it went, faster than it had ever gone before. The other kids scrambled to get out of his way.

Richard hit the ramp at full speed. The bike lifted into the air, higher than any kid had ever gone. The other kids watched in awe as it landed solidly on the wet asphalt.

Richard pedalled on, never looking back.

Stars filled the sky over the Tyler house. Richard's bike lay on its side on the front lawn as the family minivan pulled up into the driveway.

"Claire, look!" shouted Mr. Tyler. "That's Richard's bike!"

"Thank God, he's safe. I was beginning to think that we would never find him." Richard's mother breathed a deep sigh of relief.

Suddenly the tree house caught their attention at the same time. A warm yellow light glowed from within its walls.

"You think it's Richard up there?" Mr. Tyler asked. He climbed up the ladder to see. Taking one look he motioned for his wife to come up, too. Inside the tree house, an old lantern cast a yellow light over a sleeping Richard and three books nestled in his arms. "Poor baby," Richard's mum said proudly. "He looks exhausted. Shouldn't we carry him to his bed?"

"Let's let him sleep up here tonight." Richard's dad then covered his son with his jacket and turned off the lantern. Before climbing down, he kissed Richard on the cheek and whispered, "You must have had quite a trip. I'm very proud of you, son."

In the darkness of the tree house some-thing stirred—the sound of pages rustling. "It's dark out here." Horror whispered to Fantasy. "I wish there was a night-light."

"Honey, why didn't you say so?" With a blink of her wand she made the lantern flare up again, illuminating the books who were back to their old selves.

Adventure looked around and took a deep breath. "Do ye smell it? Breathe it in, mates!" He thrust his sword in the air. *"Now this be the land of Adventure!"*

Heartfelt thanks to the great storytellers and illustrators
of classic children's literature who have inspired this work.

I would like to acknowledge the following people for their help on this book:
Marge Tiritilli, without whose help the paintings in this book would not have been possible.
Charles Sikanich, the model for Richard. Scott Gustafson for too many reasons to mention.
Gary Gianni, Tom Gianni, Herb Headland, Kurt Mitchell, Phil Renaud, Lena Reynolds, Owen Reynolds,
Marc Strang, Lizzy Tiritilli, Isaiah Thompson, and Owen Thompson.

Jerry Tiritilli

KINGFISHER
An imprint of Larousse plc
Elsley House, 24-30 Great Titchfield Street
London W1P 7AD

This edition published by Kingfisher 1994
by arrangement with Turner Publishing, Inc.
2 4 6 8 10 9 7 5 3 1

ISBN: 1 85697 276 3

A CIP catalogue record for this book is available from the British Library

Editorial:
Walton Rawls, Editor
Katherine Buttler, Associate Editor
Crawford Barnett, Editorial Assistant
Walter Retan, Copy Editor

Design:
Michael J. Walsh, Vice President, Design and Production
Karen E. Smith, Art Director
Nancy Robins, Production Director
Raphael Boguslav, Lettering Illustrator
Brad Purse, Spine and Endsheet Illustrator

Printed in Italy